W9-AOV-495

ELEMENTS
OF BEING A
RANGER

by Leigh Olsen

Penguin Young Readers Licenses
An Imprint of Penguin Random House

PENGUIN YOUNG READERS LICENSES
An Imprint of Penguin Random House LLC

ISBN 9780515159875   10 9 8 7 6 5 4 3 2 1

Galvanax, the reigning champion of *Galaxy Warriors*, was furious with the Power Rangers! They had the mighty Ninja Power Stars. But he wanted the stars back on the Warrior Dome so he could steal their power!

"Get me those Power Stars!" he shouted at his underling Spinferno. "Or I'll snuff out your flames!"

"The Power Rangers will be toast, boss," Spinferno assured him. "Wait till you see what I'm gonna do to them!"

Down on Earth, it was the first day at Summer Cove High School for Brody, the Red Ranger. In the science lab, Mick, the Power Rangers' mentor, was forging brand-new Element Stars out of Ninja Steel.

"Galvanax is sending more powerful monsters," he told the Rangers. Brody handed the stars out to Calvin, Hayley, Preston, and Sarah.

"Fire, water, earth, the forest, metal," he said. "The basic elements of nature are our weapons."

But before they could practice using the Element Stars, the Power Rangers had to get to class. As the other Rangers rushed off, a ping came from Brody's Datacom.

The Datacom was connected to the Warrior Dome ship's main computer. "Show to begin at 8 a.m. Spinferno to attack at Summer Cove Plaza," it said.

"Spinferno, eh?" said Brody. He knew he didn't have any time to waste, so he raced to fight the monster—all by himself.

Spinferno's hopes of springing a surprise attack on the Rangers were dashed the moment the Red Ranger showed up.

"How did you know I was here?" Spinferno asked.

"That's for me to know and you to never find out!" said Brody.

"You're going down, Earth twerp!" Spinferno exclaimed, launching an attack on Brody. Brody couldn't keep up without the help of the other Rangers!

"Spinferno is too fast!" Brody told his Datacom. "What should I do?"

"Decrease his temperature," the Datacom suggested.

"Of course," said Brody, clicking an Element Star into his sword. "Ninja Spin! Water Attack!" Brody's sword blasted Spinferno with a jet of water, sending him flying into the sky.

"You haven't seen the last of me!" warned Spinferno as he zoomed off into the distance.

1,000,001 views

Back at school, it seemed like everyone was watching the video of the Red Ranger's epic fight with Spinferno.

Victor, the class president, wasn't too happy about it. "That video has one million and one views," he told Monty, his right-hand man. "That's one million more than mine! Those Power Rangers are stealing my popularity."

The rest of the Rangers weren't too happy, either. Brody had kept them in the dark about Spinferno! When he showed up, out of breath, Sarah let Brody know they were disappointed. "You fought a monster and didn't ask us to help?" she asked.

"Don't worry!" Brody said. "My Datacom and I handled it."

Brrrrrring! The bell for class rang. Their teacher, Mrs. Finch, gave a quick-fire quiz!

Before the rest of his classmates could do the math, Brody's Datacom gave him the answers. His hand shot up and he yelled what his Datacom said.

Mrs. Finch was impressed, but Sarah wasn't.

"Brody," she whispered, "you can't use your Datacom!"

Victor was on to him, too. "Hold it!" he shouted. "Mr. Smarty-Pants over there is cheating! Mrs. Finch, I saw the new kid use that thing on his wrist."

"What is that thingamajig you have there?" Mrs. Finch asked.

"It's my Datacom," Brody said. "It gives me answers to everything."

"I don't know about your last school," said Mrs. Finch, "but around here, that's against the rules. I don't want to see that thing again, okay?"

After class, Brody didn't even notice as his Datacom fell out of a hole in his backpack, clattering to the ground. Victor couldn't believe his good luck! "Are you thinking what I'm thinking?" he asked Monty.

"That your hair looks spectacular today?" Monty said admiringly.

"No!" Victor said. He paused. "Well, yes. But not that."

"Excuse me," Victor said to the Datacom. "I have a life-or-death question: How do I become more popular than the Power Rangers?"

"You must defeat a monster in battle," the Datacom replied.

Defeat a monster? How hard could that *possibly* be? Now Victor and Monty just had to come up with a plan.

In the cafeteria, Hayley told Brody what she really thought about his Datacom. "If it just gives you the answer, you'll never figure out how to do things on your own," she said.

"If you have a tool, you should use it," Brody said.

But before Hayley could explain why it was wrong to rely on the Datacom, Preston interrupted with some bad news. "The monster Brody fought?" Preston said. "He's back."

Brody reached for his Datacom and began to panic when he discovered it was missing. "We have to find my Datacom before we fight the monster!" he said.

"We've fought without your Datacom before," Sarah said impatiently.

"Don't worry," Brody said as his friends rushed off to fight Spinferno. "I'll be right behind you."

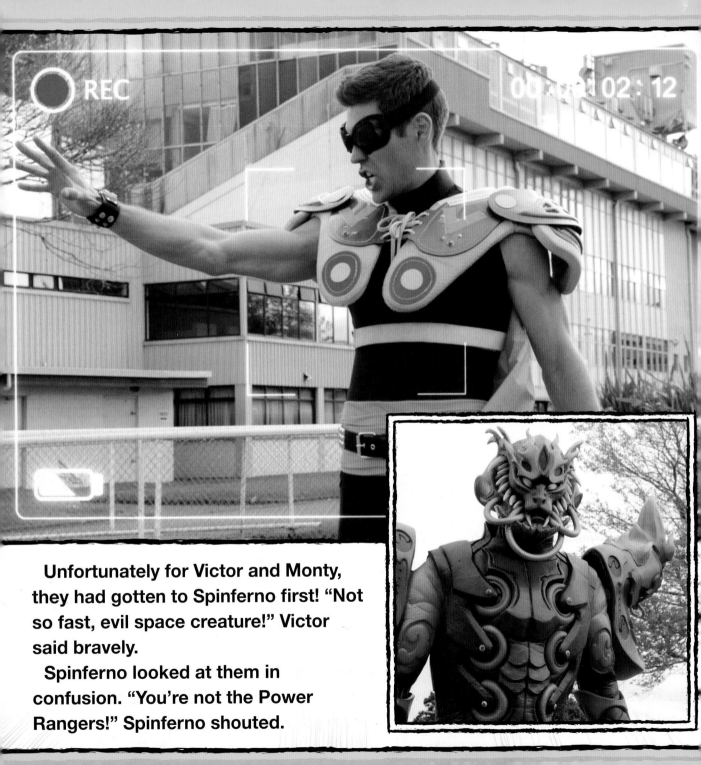

Unfortunately for Victor and Monty, they had gotten to Spinferno first! "Not so fast, evil space creature!" Victor said bravely.

Spinferno looked at them in confusion. "You're not the Power Rangers!" Spinferno shouted.

"Watch the master at work," Victor said. Monty handed him a fire extinguisher and got out his cell phone, ready to film the whole thing. "Take this!" Victor tried to spray Spinferno with the extinguisher but wound up covering *himself* in foam!

Frustrated, Spinferno blasted the Datacom out of Monty's hands. Then he tossed Victor and Monty into a fire-extinguisher-foam tornado! "Have a good trip!" Spinferno cackled as Victor and Monty spun away.

Over at the science lab, Brody was looking everywhere for his Datacom. "Are you sure you really need it?" Mick asked. "Sharing that ninja knowledge with the team this morning—that was the Datacom, right?"

"No, that was me," Brody answered.

"And escaping Galvanax's ship to save the Ninja Steel, who was that?"

"You know that was me, Mick," Brody said with a sigh.

"Look, the Datacom may give you an answer every now and then," Mick said, "but never once did it give you the courage to lead. That, my friend— that was all you."

Brody thought it over. He had to admit, Mick had a point.

"You're right," Brody said. "I don't need a Datacom. I already have everything I need. Including a great team. Thanks, Mick!" And he hurried off to help his friends in battle.

Brody found his fellow Rangers just in time to fight Spinferno. "I don't need a Datacom," he admitted. "What it takes to be a Ranger isn't in a computer. It's right here," he said, putting his hand on his heart. The other Rangers agreed.

But the Rangers still had to defeat Spinferno!
Brody locked in his Power Star and morphed into the Red Ranger.
Now all the Power Rangers were ready to fight the monster—together!
"All right, team," Brody said, leading the attack, "let's do this!"

At the sight of all five ninjas coming after him, Spinferno was on the run. "Catch me if you can!" he said with a laugh.

Luckily, Brody had a plan. "Calvin," Brody said. "Catch up with Spinferno and lure him back to Conifer Park. We'll have a trap waiting."

"Got it," Calvin said, speeding off.

Soon, Calvin tracked down Spinferno. "Yo, spin guy," Calvin said. "How about you and I have a little race? First one to Conifer Park gets my Power Star."

"A Ninja Power Star?" Spinferno said, impressed. "Let's do it! On your mark, get set, go!"

Calvin engaged his water mode Element Star, and it was on!

As Spinferno zoomed ahead, the other Rangers lay in wait at Conifer Park.

"Surprise!" said Brody, popping out from the trees and stopping Spinferno in his tracks.

Brody, Hayley, Preston, and Sarah locked in their Element Stars. "Ninja Spin!" they shouted. "Element Star! Forest Attack!"

Twisty branches shot out of each ninja's sword, wrapping around Spinferno. They held him until Calvin arrived.

"You tricked me!" Spinferno whined in defeat.

"Looks like this race is over," Calvin said.

"Element Star! Fire Attack!" shouted the Power Rangers. "Final Strike!" And the ninjas blasted Spinferno with a taste of his own fiery medicine, turning him into dust!

But the monsters watching from the Warrior Dome wanted to see a new monster take on the Power Rangers. They sent down one of the most vicious weapons in their arsenal—a Skullgator!

"That thing looks crazy!" Sarah said. What were the Power Rangers going to do now?

"Just like we've come together as a team, I think our Zords can, too," Brody said. "Ninja Steel Megazord, Combine!" And the Rangers' Zords locked together to form one gigantic armored warrior ready to take on the Skullgator!

"That thing has no hope now!" said Sarah.

"Let's teach this bad boy a lesson!" Calvin exclaimed.

Together, the Power Rangers went head-to-head with the Skullgator. But the Skullgator was no match for the Megazord's strength. It was time to do him in once and for all!

"Ninja Steel Megazord, Master Slash!" said the Power Rangers. "Final Attack!" And with one final blow, the Megazord took down the Skullgator.

"Show's over! Ninjas win!" the Power Rangers cheered.

As Galvanax watched the Power Rangers defeat him once again, he was filled with monstrous rage! "The Rangers destroyed a Skullgator, too?" he said in disbelief. He pointed to his underlings and growled, "If this happens again, you'll all be fired . . . *into the sun!*"

Later that day, Brody tracked down the other Rangers in the cafeteria.

"Guys, I'm sorry for relying on my Datacom instead of my friends," he said. "Together, we'll face a lot of different problems. The solution is always the same: teamwork."

The other Rangers accepted his apology, and Brody continued. "Galvanax cut my Datacom link to the Warrior Dome, and Mick couldn't reconnect it. But he made these Ninjacoms. Now we can communicate with each other."

Sarah, Preston, Hayley, and Calvin couldn't believe what an epic gift Brody had given them.

"These Ninjacoms connect to something even more powerful than the Warrior Dome," Preston said.

"The Ranger team," Sarah agreed.

3,559,123 views

Meanwhile, the entire school was laughing at Monty's video of Victor's embarrassing fight with Spinferno. Monty thought his friend would be angry at him for posting it. But he was totally wrong!

"You're a genius, Monty!" Victor exclaimed. "I finally have more views than the Power Rangers. They love me! They really love me!"

Brody and the other Rangers laughed. This was one fight they were willing to lose!